Other books in the same series:

Bobby, Charlton
and the Mountain

Man of the Match

Team Trouble

SOPHIE SMILEY

Illustrated by
MICHAEL FOREMAN

Andersen Press
London

The author would like to thank Jodie Mitchell and
Rose Lander from Netherhall School for all their help
in writing the blurb for this book.

First published in 2007 by
Andersen Press Limited,
20 Vauxhall Bridge Road, London SW1V 2SA
www.andersenpress.co.uk
Reprinted 2007 (twice), 2008

British Library Cataloguing in Publication Data available
ISBN 978 1 84270 684 8

Printed in the UK by CPI Bookmarque, Croydon, CR0 4TD

For my sisters,
Mary-Clare, Kate and Rachel – S.S.

Chapter 1

'Come on, you reds!' Dad yelled.

Wembley balanced boots on his head, Striker kicked a cushion, Bobby shouted, 'Save,' and Mum blew her whistle. It's always mad at our house on match days.

Everyone was ready. Everyone except Semi.

My middle brother was still in his pyjamas, sprawled across the sofa.

Bobby tugged his hand. 'Get dress' NOW,' he ordered.

But Semi just flicked through the channels, changing from a football match to a cartoon. Something was wrong. Very wrong. No one in our house ever switches the football off. And we always go to the match together – like Dad says, we're a team.

Mum and Dad exchanged glances, as if they knew something, but weren't telling.

Nobody spoke as we left. There was a big hole where Semi should have been.

Dad sang louder than usual, as if to fill the gap.

Semi wasn't around to tell jokes, so Bobby started: 'Knock knock.'

'Who's there?'

'Football!'

'Football who?'

'Football hoooligan!'

When our team won 3-0, and the

crowd went wild, I thought of
Semi. I couldn't remember him
missing a match before, ever.

Next day, when I got home from
school the house was strangely
quiet. Mum wasn't singing, or
dribbling a football round the
kitchen. She was staring into
space. My big brother, Striker,
made her a cup of tea. I curled up
in a corner with a football
magazine. If I listened, I'd find out
what the matter was.

'I think Semi's got your old
disease,' Mum said.

'What's that?' asked Striker.

'TT syndrome,' she replied,
ruffling his hair.

TT syndrome – what was that? I've always known my brother, Bobby, has Down's syndrome. That's why he goes to a different school from me. A special school. But he's not ill or anything, and he's a brilliant goalie. Now it looked like we had another syndrome in the family. This new one was really serious: it meant not liking football!

Chapter 2

Semi's TT syndrome didn't get better. It got worse. He wouldn't get up in the morning. He shouted at Bobby, and he started spending time in the bathroom. Semi hated baths; he never washed. But now he was locking himself away for hours.

'Come out NOW!' Bobby ordered. He missed playing with Semi.

'Go away!' Semi growled.

Bobby didn't know about the TTs, but he realised that something was wrong, and he moped for the old Semi – the one who told him daft jokes and wrestled with him.

One day, Semi arrived late to the meal. His hair was covered in gel, and sticking out.

'Look – a jelly hedgehog,' Dad joked.

Mum shot him a warning glance. I was getting used to her noisy, silent stares.

13

'They'll be playing the new striker tomorrow.' Dad tried to bring Semi out of his scowls. 'D'you reckon he'll score?'

'Whatever,' Semi shrugged.

The meal table went quiet. Our house is never quiet.

Semi hunched over his plate, shovelling food in.

'Don't eat with your mouth open,' Dad said.

'Stop nagging me!' Semi flung down his knife and fork, slamming the door as he stormed out.

Dad stood up. 'Semi . . .' he roared.

'Shhh,' Mum stopped him. 'Let it go – he needs lots of TLC at the moment.'

'Yup – plenty of TLC for the old TTs.' Dad looked fed up.

Well, I was fed up with grown-ups talking in code.

'Pass the TK,' I said, pointing at the ketchup, 'and the S and P.'

I wasn't going to be left out.

Bobby plopped a sausage in the water jug, flicked a dollop of mashed potato at the ceiling, and muttered 'ABC an' BBC'. Then he

ate with his mouth wide open, deliberately putting out his tongue and showing us his half-eaten food.

'Bobby!' Mum snapped, flashing a yellow card. 'Any more of that, and you'll be sent off.'

''S not fair,' Bobby grumbled. 'Give Semi a red card.'

His face drooped till his nose pinged the gravy. Lifting his head, he grinned at me, then bobbed down for another go.

'That's enough,' a deep voice growled.

''Nuff B-U-M,' Bobby muttered, before cramming three forkfuls into his mouth. If he was going to be sent off, he wasn't

going to leave any of his chicken
on the pitch!

Strangely, Mum didn't bring
out the red card. She looked
worried and a bit far away.

While I was washing up, I heard
her talking softly with Dad. The
word 'doctor' set my ears jangling.

Later, Mum and Semi
went out. Semi was
wearing dark
glasses, his hair
flopped over his
face like a pair
of curtains. He
was all hunched
over. Whatever it
was, it was getting worse.

When they came home, I saw

him take a packet of pills from the shopping bag and slip them into his pocket.

'What're you staring at?' he snapped.

'Nothing.' I sloped off into the garden. Kicking a football around usually makes me feel better.

But the funny feeling didn't go away. It grew.

So next day at school, I sneaked a look in the big dictionary. First, I searched for 'Sindrome'. Whatever Semi had, it was something bad. Sins were bad. But it wasn't under sin. Eventually, I found the word under S Y N, and read: 'Combination of behaviour and emotions.' Well, Semi was certainly

showing some odd behaviour
recently. But then, Dad and Mum
have some odd behaviour, and
they didn't have syndromes. At
least, I didn't think they did. It
was confusing. I read the next bit:
'Symptoms of a disease,' it said.
That sounded more serious.
Doctor. Pills. Semi must be
poorly. What if he was really ill?

Chapter 3

I kept looking out for signs of
Semi's illness. But it wasn't like a
normal illness, when you go to
bed for a few days and then get
better. Instead, he came down
stairs, lay on the sofa, and grunted
at people.

'D'you want to read my football
magazine?'

'Ooof.'

'I want to watch the other

channel.'

'Noyoucan't. Oof.'

'Come to the park with us,
Semi.'

'Naagarroffanleavemealone.
Oof!'

One day Mum took him
shopping. When we're poorly
Mum buys us little treats – drinks
and comics. But Semi came back

with a whole bag of new clothes.
So whatever it was, TT must be
more serious than chickenpox.
The clothes were awful. We all
wear football shirts, but Semi's
new shirt was was covered in
flowers – ugh! Dad got out his
watering can and started to
sprinkle the flowery shirt. Mum
shooed him away. He stomped out
like a player who's been sent off.

Semi's bedroom changed, as
well as his clothes. All the football
posters came down, and up went
pictures of girls in bikinis.

He's always loved swimming
(not like me) but when Mum
suggested he take Bobby to the
pool, he just grunted.

'Don'wanto. Oof.'

'Go on, it'll do you good – and you, Charlie.' Mum swooshed us all out of the house.

At the pool, Bobby made straight for the diving board. He bounced up and down, then launched himself into space, arms and legs flying. As he flew off the board, I threw a ball at him. He kicked it back, yelled, 'Goal!' and disappeared into a mass of bubbles.

I liked this game – it meant I didn't have to get into the water at all. But after a while I got bored, and wanted to read a book. Semi was lying in the sun, so I went to sit near him. A dripping Bobby

followed and gave Semi a wet hug.

'Geroff,' he growled.

'Play polo?' Bobby asked.

Semi's brilliant at water polo,
and usually he and Bobby play for
hours. But today Bobby got the
'Go away' treatment.

So he played on his own for a
bit, before crumpling next to
Semi. Like me, he was confused.

And cross.

Semi lay on the grass, not reading, not talking, not doing anything. And he wouldn't take off that horrible shirt. I tried to ignore him. But Bobby kept fluttering round with questions – 'Wha' you doin'?' 'Why?' 'Why don' you want to swim?'

Perhaps he'd become allergic to

water, I thought. Naomi in my class is allergic to nuts. And Daniel has a special pen in case he gets stung by bees. But if Semi was allergic to water, why did he spend hours in the bathroom? It didn't make sense.

Bobby got fed up. A few minutes later, he crept towards Semi carrying a cup of water. He lifted up the flowery shirt, and was just about to pour water onto his back when he shrieked and ran away.

'Ugh! Yukky, yukky!' Bobby pointed in disgust.

Semi leaped to his feet, furious. He picked Bobby up, chucked him into the pool, and stormed off.

I stared after him. So, the secret TT disease was on his back. Bobby had seen it. And it was horrible. More horrible than I'd ever imagined.

Chapter 4

Bobby was upset. He knew that Semi was really angry, and kept trying to make it better.

'Wanta sweet?' he offered.
'Carry your bag, Semi?'

'Knock knock who's there?'

But Semi ignored him all the way home.

When we got back, Bobby kept trying to be nice to Semi. 'Cuppa tea?' he asked. 'Borrow my goalie video?' But Semi didn't even look up. Then he offered Semi a football sticker – not just any sticker, but his best one, the one with his goalie hero, Will Brooks. 'For you . . .' he said.

Semi just grunted and pushed him away. Finally, Bobby buried his head in his crossed legs and wouldn't say a word. Perhaps he was catching TT syndrome too, I thought. Maybe we'd all get it, and everyone in the house would stop talking, and just grunt. Perhaps tourists would come and visit The House of Grunts.

I kicked a ball around listlessly till tea time.

When Bobby sat down he had

his 'I've been up to something' look on his face. Mum usually notices it straight away, and I waited for her to tackle him. But she just dished out the mashed potato – one scoop on each plate, and then one dollop in the gold-fish bowl.

'Mum!'

'Oh, silly me – I was miles away'.

Goal Fish nudged the potato ball down the tank.

'He's making a run on goal,' I said.

No one laughed. Then the door burst open. Semi grabbed Bobby, and pulled him roughly onto the floor. Semi, my gentle, dreamy brother, started hitting Bobby.

Mum blew a whistle. 'Stop at once,' she said, flashing a red card.

Semi gasped and yelled, 'He's scribbled all over my pictures. I hate this place and I hate this family. I'm leaving!'

He stormed out.

'Rude boy,' Bobby muttered, and scuttled under the table.

Mum and Dad exchanged glances, and I wondered what they'd do. They hate fighting, and always try to teach me to hold my head up high, and walk away when I'm angry. But they'd never had to say that to Semi.

I expected Dad to go after Semi and be really fierce, but Mum gave him one of her signals and he stayed where he was.

'Bobby!' she said. 'Upstairs.

Now.'

I sneaked up behind them, and peeped round the door as Mum marched Bobby into Semi's room.

Bobby hung his head as Mum pointed to the posters. All the smiling, bikini-clad girls now had football shirts and bobble hats. Felt pens were scattered over the floor. He'd even pinned a smelly old sock onto one girl's belly button.

There was a long silence. Then a great crashing sound came from the garden. We all rushed to the window. A bucket flew out of the shed. An old bike wheel rolled after it, and wobbled its way into the cabbages. Dad stood and

watched as the entire contents of
his beloved shed flew onto the
grass. He looked shocked, like a
ref who's just had a ball kicked in
his face.

An arm reached round the shed
door, and a notice appeared:
'Privet! Keep Out!'

We all stared at each other,
stunned.

Semi had left home.

Chapter 5

Poor Semi. He was ill, and alone. I remembered a nature programme I'd seen, when the old animal left the herd to die.

I tried to imagine how I'd feel if I was really poorly, and someone drew on my football posters, and I had to go and sleep in a shed with snails and spiders. I wanted my brother back, and I wanted him better. Mum always says, 'When

you're sad, try and think of
something that will make someone
else happy.'

My piggy bank stared at me. I'd
got just enough saved to buy the
last footballer for my team. I really
wanted that model.

But Semi was poorly.

I could have the whole set.

But what if Semi was ill, really
ill?

I rattled Piggy. All my pocket
money. And it was Bobby who'd

scribbled on the posters, not me –
why should I do anything?

Piggy seemed to shake his head
– as if he was telling me that our
family team was more important
than a plastic one. Reluctantly, I
carried the money box out to the
shed.

I pictured his smiling face. I'd
be the one to bring him home. I'd
help him get better.

I knocked on the door, and
said, 'Semi, here's some money to
buy new posters.'

'Gerrroff and goaway!' Semi
yelled.

Chapter 6

That was it. He could go on a free transfer to Dirty Shed United for all I cared!

I stormed inside. It was worse than the day we lost the cup final. I'd tried really hard to be kind, and he'd slammed the door in my face!

Well, he'd asked for it.

'Mum,' I began, 'we need a baby.'

She spluttered tea everywhere.

'A new midfielder.'

Mum rattled her cup down.
'There's only one midfielder in
this family,' she said fiercely, 'and
that's Semi! He's my middle child,
and right now he's in the middle
of some troubles.'

'Piggy 'n middle, piggy 'n
muddle,' Bobby sang from under
the sofa.

'That's enough from you, young man – it's time you went and said sorry. Off you go. You can take him his tea.'

Bobby picked up Semi's plate. Then he stopped. He was trying to decide something. Finally, he sighed, took the lolly from his mouth, and popped it on top of the potato.

A hand reached out from the shed door, and took the plate.

There was a grunt, 'Oof.' The door closed. Then it opened again. A lolly flew out and hit Bobby – smack – on the nose!

Chapter 7

Semi stayed in the shed. He only came indoors to lock himself in the bathroom for hours. And more hours. Then, smelling like a flower shop, he'd leave. He never said where he was going or when he'd be back, and I could tell that bothered Mum, even though she didn't say anything.

'Me come?' Bobby asked each time.

And each time he was greeted with a big 'NO'. So Bobby would go and mope under the sofa. I tried to coax him out to play football, but he just shook his head and buried his face in the carpet. I ended up all alone, kicking a ball against the back wall. It felt like I'd lost two brothers.

One day Semi went out.

'An' me?' Bobby tried.

Semi left without answering,

and I saw a new look on Bobby's
face. He lay under the sofa, but his
eyes peeped out from between his
fingers. He was up to something. I
went into the kitchen and listened.
Soft footsteps made their way to
the front door. It closed very
quietly. I peered out, and watched
Bobby tiptoeing down the road
like a pantomime villain, as Semi
disappeared into the distance.

Jumping into my trainers, I
rushed after them.

The sky darkened.

I jumped from tree to tree. Semi kept stopping, looking round nervously. A cat darted out. Semi jumped. What was turning my big, brave brother into this jittery ghost? A car with black windows snaked up to the curb. It slid away like a shark, and Semi scuttled down an alley. He started to run. This wasn't just an illness. He was frightened of something.

I couldn't see Bobby. I froze.

A group approached, and Semi dived out of sight. They passed me, and I recognised them from Semi's class. Why was he hiding from his schoolmates?

There was a rumble of thunder,

and heavy rain drops began to fall.
Dark spots appeared on Semi's
shirt, merging and clinging to his
hunched shape. Something
screeched from the bushes.
Branches whipped my face and
the path became a black tunnel.
Semi moved faster. He looked
around again, then darted through
a gap in the hedge. Seconds later,
I squeezed after him, into the
park. It was empty. Deserted. If
someone attacked him, no one
would hear his screams. Lightning
slashed the sky, and he ran
towards it, taking great loping
strides as if he was being chased. I
darted from bush to bush, losing
him and glimpsing him again as he

sprinted like the wind. There was just one, solitary figure in the bandstand, something dark pulled over its head. Was it armed? Semi pounded forwards. He raised his arms towards the figure. Thunder rolled around the park, and the two shapes fell together, and disappeared from sight. Someone had grabbed him.

Chapter 8

Who'd got Semi? And where was
Bobby? I charged forward.

A bloodcurdling noise erupted
from the hollyhocks.

A head shot up.

'OOOooh – kissy, kissy, kissy!'
Bobby's grin appeared from a
flowerbed.

Semi sprang to his feet, his face
a red card. I could feel his glare
fifty metres away.

Sitting beside him, surprised and fluffy, was a girl. A girly girl!

Looking up, she fluttered, and reached out for Semi. She was holding my brother's hand! Staring up at him with a silly, soppy expression on her face.

'Play foo'ball?' Bobby's voice wobbled.

'Go away!' Semi hissed.

Bobby put his head on one side and held out the ball.

'Foo'ball, please?' His small voice floated from the flowers.

The wispy, golden hair twirled towards Semi and back to Bobby.

'P'ease?'

'Go home!' Semi pointed furiously at the gate.

'I'll play, Bobby,' I tried.

'Semi . . .' Bobby wailed.

'Come on. Let's go.' Semi tugged the girl. She tottered beside him for a few steps in her wibbly wobbly shoes. Then she stopped.

'Hold this,' she thrust a sparkly handbag at Semi and teetered towards the flowerbed. Bobby held out the football and said, 'For you,' as if it was a present.

She took the ball and trip trapped onto the pitch, nearly falling off her stupid shoes. She tried to kick but missed. I smiled. Then Bobby passed her another one, really gently. She sliced it badly.

'Goo' girl,' he said when she returned it, and then asked, 'Name?'

'Primrose,' she replied.

'Premier,' Bobby nodded, passing the ball back to her. Her heels slipped down into the mud. She unstrapped the shoes, put them neatly together, and skipped into a puddle. Clumsily, she kicked the ball back to Bobby, squelching and giggling across the muddy pitch.

Semi and I stood on the touchline and stared at each other. Finally, Bobby said, 'Tea time, Premier!' and taking her by the hand, he led the way to our house.

Semi picked up her shoes and

sulked along behind. I joined him,
taking his free hand. 'She'll never
go out with me again if she sees
our house and you lot,' Semi said
miserably. I didn't like the way he
called us 'you lot', but he had
spoken to me, in real words and

without a single grunt. And he
hadn't pushed my hand away.

'Don't worry,' I said, 'she's
nice.'

And for the first time in weeks,
he smiled at me.

We reached our house, and
Mum opened the door. A cabbage
sailed over her head, and a rather
startled Primrose Premier caught
it.

'Goo' save,' Bobby said, and led
her inside.

Chapter 9

It was match day again. Everyone was getting ready – well, everyone except Semi.

The door bell rang, and Bobby ran to open it, yelling, 'Primrose Premier!'

Tugging her hand, he dragged her through to the garden.

'Penalties?' he asked, handing her a football.

Bobby usually does penalty

practice with me. I kicked a cushion at the wall. Nobody even noticed me.

Mum wandered in singing, 'Football's coming home, it's coming . . .'

She gazed happily at Bobby and Primrose in the garden, then said, 'Semi's a lucky lad.'

'Is he?' I looked up, startled.

'Yes,' Mum smiled. 'She's a lovely girl. You wanted a new midfielder. I think she's a great new signing, don't you?'

'She kicks like a girl,' I said. Then added, 'And I bet he hasn't told her about his illness.'

'What illness?' Mum looked puzzled.

'You know. The doctor. All that stuff. You and Dad never telling him off. His yukky back . . .'

'Oh, Charlie,' she laughed, 'that was just spots, acne. Lots of teenagers get it. It's nearly gone now.'

'Oh, I thought . . . I was worried he might . . .' my voice wobbled.

Then Dad appeared yelling

'Nearly match time – come on, you reds.'

'And yellows,' Bobby added, thundering upstairs and shouting, 'Get up, Semi slug-a-bed!'

Primrose trotted behind him, saying, 'Hurry up, Semi – you promised you'd take me to my first match.'

Striker came in, grinning, and said, 'Semi seems to be getting over the TTs.'

'What's that?' I demanded.

'Oh, just teenage troubles, dear,' Mum said. 'You'll have them too.'

'I won't. I won't ever stop liking football!' I said.

'I'm afraid you will,' Mum smiled, 'and then you'll need some extra TLC, just like Semi.'

'You're doing it again!'

'What?' asked Mum.

'Talking in code. What's TLC?'

'Tender Loving Care,' Mum, Dad and Striker said together.

'Youngest children need that too,' I grumped, 'and a syndrome. I don't want to be the only person in this house without a syndrome.'

'An' me,' said Bobby.

'Bobby, you can have BIGS,' said Mum. 'Best In Goal!'

'Charlie's got BOGSS,' Dad added. 'Brilliant Only Girl Striker Syndrome!'

'Football, BIGS?' I asked.

'Yes, BOGSS,' Bobby replied.

'Wait for us!' Semi and Primrose bounded out. 'We'll give you a game!'

About the Author

Sophie Smiley was born in a Dominican monastery – she says she had a very happy childhood surrounded by Fra Angelicos and Ethopian priests! She now teaches English and is also a staff member of Forest School Camps, working with both the able and those with learning difficulties. She is married and has two children and they all live in Cambridge.

About the Illustrator

Michael Foreman is one of the most talented and popular creators of children's books today. He has won the Kate Greenaway Medal for illustration twice and his highly acclaimed books are published all over the world. He is married, has three sons and divides his time between St Ives in Cornwall and London.

Have you read the other books about Bobby, Charlton, and their football-mad family?

Man of the Match

Bobby and Charlie are off to summer camp. As soon as Bobby sees Paul, he insists on being best friends with him, even though Paul hides under his parka. Of course Bobby insists on playing football with Paul whatever the planned activity really is. Charlie has her work cut out to keep track of them – and she has a big challenge of her own, too – a relay race over water, and she's petrified!

Bobby, Charlton and the Mountain

Bobby, wants a football kit for the Queen's visit to his school! Money-making muddles, a beastly bully, and a breathtaking penalty shoot-out lead to a VERY unexpected meeting . . . !

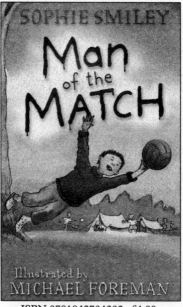

ISBN 9781842704202 £4.99

ISBN 9781842701782 £3.99